WRITERS REPUBLIC

PRINCESS FERMINITY

BRIANNA WARNKE

WRITERS REPUBLIC L.L.C.
515 Summit Ave. Unit R1
Union City, NJ 07087, USA

Website: *www.writersrepublic.com*
Hotline: *1-877-656-6838*
Email: *info@writersrepublic.com*

Ordering Information:
Quantity sales. Special discounts are available on quantity purchases by corporations, associations, and others. For details, contact the publisher at the address above.

Library of Congress Control Number: 2021920724
ISBN-13:   978-1-63728-977-8   [Paperback Edition]
                  978-1-63728-978-5   [Digital Edition]

Rev. date: 10/18/2021

DEDICATION

I would like to dedicate this book to my father James Arthur Gibbons III. He has recently passed away and with his passing, I was able to finish this book and have the courage to try and get it published. I thank him so much for all he has done for me in my life. I love you daddy and will always love you.

You have made me who I am today and never judged me for my faults. I love you always and forever. I would also like to thank my husband and father to our children Kenneth James Warnke.

For all your support during this long process. If it weren't for you, I could not have done this I love you and thank you so much.

Once upon a time, there was a King and Queen who ruled a small kingdom called Morane. The King was named King Leabou. The queen was named Queen Azailia. King Leabou and Queen Azailia were very kind to the people. So everyone loved them. The only problem they had was they had no children to take over the kingdom when they were gone. They had no luck. They tried but would fail. They began to lose hope and thought it would never happen.

Then one day, Queen Azallia was not feeling very well; she had been sick off and on for a few months. So they sent for the doctor to examine her. When he arrived, he gave her a thorough examination. The doctor finished examing Queen Azailla. King Leabou came in. "I have found something, it looks like you are going to have a baby, and you are due in two months." Queen Azalia and King Leabou were so excited. They could not imagine their dreams were finally going to come true.

They called all the staff, and they began to work. The team worked for two months until it was time for the party. There were walls with colorful silk fabrics. There were long tables lined with beautiful tablecloths and flowers. There were twelve long tables with mounds of food from around the world, all the queen's favorite dishes. The clock struck 7:00 pm. They opened the castle gates.

Carriages of all shapes and sizes entered the gates and rode up to the castle doors. The guests who exited the carriages had on their most delicate gowns and suits. When all the guests entered the ballroom for the first moment, they were in awe of what they saw. As the king and queen entered the room for the first time, the queen was pleased with how everything looked; she kissed the king. "Well done, I could not be more pleased." They went to their table at the head of the room, sat down, and enjoyed their meal.

The queen loved to dance. She grabbed the king's hand and pulled him out to the dance floor. They began to dance. They danced and danced and danced until it began to get late. The queen was feeling very tired and weak and started getting pains in her side. So she went to sit down and have some water. That did not help. The pain was getting stronger now and coming more often.

The King got nervous and called for the doctor. It was lucky for them he was in attendance at the ball. The doctor came over and examined the queen. "Well, my dear," he said in a low tone, "you're in labor." "What," she said in a high voice. "But it's not time I have another month." "I'm sorry, your baby girl wants out now." King Leabou asked for some blankets and pillows to try and Queen Azaila as comfortable as possible given the circumstances.

Queen Azalia was doing great. The labor only lasted about an hour and a half. Then she was born. She was a beautiful baby girl. The King picked up his beautiful daughter and said, "Welcome to the world Princess Ferminity." Ferminity meant beauty. It was the perfect fit for his beautiful daughter. As he looked down at her little face, she looked up at him and cooed. His heart melted, and he began to cry. He kissed her cheek and said, "I love you, my sweet little angel."

They got Queen Azallia up to her room in the castle, and she fell right to sleep. The Housekeepers got everything from the party and delivery all cleaned up. The castle was back to its quiet self.

A few months went by. Ferminity was growing beautifully. Her favorite time was when Queen Azallia would take her to the library and read to her. She loved the sound of her mother's voice. She would lay on her lap while her mother sat in a rocking chair in the library. She would read to Ferminity for hours on end. Ferminity would just lay there listening to any kind of story. It did not matter Ferminity would listen.

A few years went by. Princess Ferminity grew to be a beautiful young woman. Every day Princess Ferminity would get up and go to the library, grab a new book, and head outside to read. She found a large cave behind a waterfall that she had turned into her private hideaway. It had a kitchen, a library, a bedroom, and even a bathroom. It was her spot.

One day, she woke up extra early and went to the library to get a book to take with her to her place behind the waterfall. As she searched the shelves, she found a book she had not read yet. It was titled, "The Man Who Knew Too Little," By Zhauck Munroe. Then she went to the kitchen to collect a snack to take with her. She put some bread and ham and cheese in a bag, then she put some crackers in a bag and got two bottles of water. She put all the items in a picnic basket and headed toward the stables to collect a picnic blanket.

When she arrived at the stable, there was a surprise there. A young man was hired as the new Stable Hostler. His name was Christian. He was in charge of all the duties and all the animals in the stable. He was brushing one of the horse's manes. She went up to him and said, "Hello, are there any blankets in here I could use for a picnic?" He said yes, he got one out for her. She put it in her basket and said, "Thank you, are there any horses ready to ride?" He got Shera out of the stall and said, "Would you like me to saddle her up for you"? She said, "no thanks, I think I can manage." So she saddled up Sherra and headed out.

Christian stayed behind and began his duties. As Ferminity rode off, she thought she saw something flying toward her. She slowed down to get a better look; as it was coming closer toward them, Sherra became spooked and hurtled herself in the air. As her legs rose in the air Ferminity was knocked to the ground and knocked unconscious. Christian, who was watching from the stables, got on the first horse he saw Midnight and raced to help her. When he reached her, she was still unconscious, and her head was bleeding on one side. Christian picked her up, laid her on Midnight's back, and walked her to his cottage by the stables. He laid her on the couch and went to get a damp cloth and some bandages to clean the wound.

When he came back, Ferminity was coming around. He went to her side and began wiping the blood from her face.

"Awe," she screeched, "that hurts." "I'm sorry, but you had a bad fall, and I need to clean the wound before it gets infected." She reached up to feel her head and said, "what happened"? "You were riding Shera, and something came toward you and spooked her. She jumped up, and you fell off." "What was it"? "I don't know exactly. I could not see very well from where I was." "Well, thank you for your help. I need to go home; my parents are probably worried and looking for me by now." "You're right; I'll take you home." When they got home, it was late in the afternoon. Princess Ferminity was exhausted, so she decided to take a nap. When she woke up, it was the next day. She headed out to the stables. When she arrived there, Christian was there brushing Shera's mane.

As she entered, she said, "thank you for your help yesterday. I appreciate it." "You're welcome, anytime," he said. "Where are you off too"? "I'm heading out for a picnic. Would you like to join me"? "Yes, if you don't mind"? So Christian put a saddle on Thunder's back and one on Shera's back. Then they headed out of the barn.

Ferminity took Christian to her favorite picnic spot that was in a clearing surrounded by flowers. Next to the waterfall. She had never brought anyone here before, but she trusted Christian for some reason. When she looked into his eyes, he made her feel safe. Like she could always trust him. She laid the blanket out and set out the food, and they began to eat. They talked about their favorite things to eat. They spoke about each other's favorite things to do and each other's hopes and dreams. As they sat there speaking to one another, an apparition of a unicorn appeared to them. They hear a strange neigh and are startled. So they got up and walked toward the sound. They see the unicorn. It is was surprised by their movement and begins to walk in the opposite direction. They begin to follow it. As they were walking, they stopped suddenly because they heard a strange noise. They look to the left and see something all tangled up in what looked like string and barbed wire and dirt and leaves. As they move closer, they know that it is a black horse.

Christian got his pocket knife out and began removing the wire and the string from the horse. There were many scrapes and cuts on the horse. They decided to take him back to the stable to help him and clean the wounds. Christian carefully tied what was left of the string around his neck and led him back to the barn. Femininity watched as Christian carefully removed the wire and the leaves and cleaned the horse. He bandaged all the wounds and led him to an open stall. He gave him some fresh hay and put clean water in the trough.

When Ferminity saw the care Christian took to help this animal, she felt closer to him than any other person. She saw the compassion and love he gave the creature he just met, and she knew she could trust him. He made her feel safe and secure. When she looked into his eyes, she knew she could always trust him. When he finished cleaning all the wounds and placing all the bandages on him. They took him out to the corral. Then they decided to give him a name they called him Thunder.

A few weeks went by, and Christian and Ferminity started dating exclusively. Every day Ferminity would get up early and head out to the barn to see Thunder. Christian would be in the stables working when she would enter. Christian would come to help her get Thunder's saddles on. Then he would put Shera's saddle on, and they would take long rides together. One day they were riding, and they went to her spot behind the waterfall. They went into the library part and picked out a book and would sit down, and he would read to her. She loved listening to him read. He read three books to her.

As he finished reading the third book, she looked up at him and smiled. He looked down at her and said, "I love you" It was the first time either one had said those words to each other. She was shocked to hear him say it. She had been feeling something for a very long time and was afraid to say it herself. But he said it first. So she smiled and said, "I love you too." Then they kissed the deepest, most passionate kiss either of them had experienced. The passion between them rose during the kiss, and they knew it would last forever.

It began to get late, so Christian and Ferminity decided to go back to the castle. They walked out of the hideaway and to the horses. Christian picked up Ferminity and placed her on Thunder's back. Then he got on Shera's back, and they held each other's hand as they rode back to the stables talking and laughing.

A few days went by, and Ferminity had not seen Christian for a couple of days now. She went out to the stables. He was there giving some freshwater to Thunder and Shera. She went and got Thunder's saddle and got him ready to ride. She got on him and rode off to her favorite spot behind the waterfall. She grabbed a book and began to read. She read a story about a prince and princess who were madly in love with one another. She read and read for five hours. Then all of a sudden, Christian walked in and said, "what are you doing"? She said, "I am reading a book." He said, "What are you reading"? She said, "I am reading a story about a prince and princess who were madly in love with one another." "Is it a good book?" he asked. "Yes, It is; it is a wonderful book." "Would you like to read one? You can read one if you would like." "Ok, which one"? She said, "pick one whichever you like." So he picked one called "The King Who Liked no Little." By Sonya Bacdone. They read and read until they had finished their books. They left the hideaway and went home.

A few months went by, and Christian and Ferminity were spending a lot of time together. Almost every day, they would go riding or go for long walks. Sometimes they would sit on the castle grounds and talk. They loved spending time together. Then one day, Christian asked. "Will you go on a picnic with me"? She said "yes," so they got on Thunder and Shera and rode off. They went to a particular place deep in the forest. It was a beautiful meadow surrounded by big lush trees. They spread out a big blanket to sit on for the picnic. They sat down and talked for a while about their hopes and dreams for the future. They ate their lunch. When they finished, they laid down and watched the clouds move in the breeze. Then they fell asleep. When they woke up, Christian got on one knee, pulled out a small box from his pocket, and said: "Ferminity, I love you so much. I know I don't come from much, but I know my heart is full when I am with you. Will you marry me?"

"Well, let me think about it, Ok I've thought about it, Yes I will marry you." "I love you." "I love you too." Christian slid the ring on her finger and kissed her. Then they left to go and speak with the King and Queen to ask their permission to marry their daughter.

When they arrived at the stables, they put their saddles away and the horses in the coral. Then Ferminity and Christian walked together up to the castle. Queen Azailla was pacing by the door. "Where have you been? I have been worried sick". "Sorry, mother, I didn't mean to make you worry we were having a good time, and I lost track of time." "You should have checked in with me, young lady." "I'm sorry, mother, but I have some news, and I want you to be the first one to know." So Ferminity told her mother, "Christian said he loves me, and I love him so much I want to be with him always." Queen Moraine was shocked and excited at the same time, excited because her daughter had found someone to love. Shocked by the fact it is a stable boy that has stolen her heart. "Well, I am happy for you, honey. What are you going to do now?" "Well, we would like your permission to be married."

Queen Azalia looked at the sincerity in Ferminity's eyes and knew she truly loved him. She said, "I think we all need to sit down with your father and discuss this rationally.

Because I know what he will do if we spur it on him, he will have Christian hung for treason or some other made-up excuse. So let's plan on having dinner tomorrow night to let him know what is going on. Tell Christian to be here at 5 pm sharp." Ferminity said, "thank you so much mother for understanding." "Don't thank me yet; we'll have to wait for your father's reaction." She kissed Ferminity's head, and Ferminity ran up the stairs to bed. She was so excited she could not sleep. She imagined what her life would be like with Christian by her side. She couldn't wait to start her life with him.

She woke up extra early the following day and went outside to find Christian. He was in the barn. She walked up behind him and said, "I have some news. My parents would like you to come to dinner tonight so they can get to know you." He said, "Ok," and they spent the rest of the day together. It was getting close to dinner time, and Ferminity went back to the castle so she could dress for dinner, and Christian went to his cottage to get cleaned up and ready for dinner. He walked up to the castle doors with a bouquet for the queen in his hand. Ferminity was waiting outside for him. He was not nervous at all, but Ferminity was terrified. She feared her father would disapprove and would not let them get married. When they came into the dining hall, the King and Queen were sitting there waiting for them.

Christian handed the queen the bouquet. "Thank you, Christian. They are lovely." She put them in a vase on the table. Then Ferminity and Christian sat down. The queen started the conversation. "So Christian, how do you like working in the stables?" "I love it. I have always enjoyed working with animals; I've been working with them since I was a little boy. My father was a Station manager when I was growing up and, I loved working beside him taking care of horses". Christian never faltered; he answered every question the King and Queen had for him. It began to get late. Queen Azailla winked at Christian to let him know it was time to ask the question. So he said, "your majesties, I would like to ask your permission to marry Ferminity? I love her with all my heart, and I always will." Before the King could answer, Queen Azailla said, "of course you can. We both give you our blessing, don't we, darling?" The queen rose from her seat, walked over to Femininity, and kissed her on the cheek. The King rose, and Christian grabbed Ferminitys hand in fear. He walked to them and kissed Ferminity on the cheek, and said, "If this is the man that makes you happy and you would like to spend your life with him. I give you my blessing." Ferminity was so happy she stood up, kissed her father, and said, "thank you, daddy, I am so happy." Her mother kissed her on the cheek and kissed Christian on the cheek and said, "congratulations to you both." Christian thanked the King and Queen again for the meal, and he and Ferminity walked out of the room to the castle's entrance. She kissed him goodnight and said, "I will see you tomorrow. I love you so much." Christian went back to his cottage and went to sleep. Ferminity went upstairs to go to bed. She had the best dreams of her life.

The next day Ferminity went outside to find Christian. She went to his cottage to see if he was there. She went to the stable to see if he was there. She looked all around then finally she saw him asleep under the horse's hay. He had fallen asleep when he went to work that morning. She ran over to him and said, "wake up" he woke up and said, "Hello, did I sleep here all night"? She said, "Yes, I guess so. I'm not sure when you came out here." "Well, I better be going." So she got Thunder all ready and kissed Christian on the cheek, and left the stables. And Christian began all his work for the day.

Queen Azalia was so excited about the wedding. When she woke up that morning, she immediately began planning her daughter's wedding. They worked and worked on everything for ten months. Finally, they were finished, everything looked beautiful.

Ferminity went to a small ballroom with her mother. Seamstress Alanea came to create her wedding dress. When they finished, it looked sensational. It was a beautiful light tan whitish color. It had a long train down the back and a beautiful veil. The dress was long past her feet and was very heavy to carry as she walked up to the mirror. As the queen looked at her daughter, she began to cry with joy. She looked exquisite, elegant, and simply beautiful. "This is the one," the queen said with a huge smile on her face.

The next thing they did was pick out dresses for the maid of honor and all the rest of the dresses and suits for everyone else at the wedding party.

It was the day before the wedding, and everyone was nervous and excited all at once. Except for the King, of course. He still didn't like the fact that his only daughter was going to marry a stable manager.

Ferminity went down to check on Thunder and Shera. When she got to the stable, she heard voices. She went in, and she saw two people lying on the ground and rolling. It was her best friend, Suri, and Christian. "AWEEEE" she screamed and ran back to the castle to find her mother and tell her the wedding was off. When she saw her, she was out of breath from running and crying. Queen Azalia asked, "What is the matter, honey? Why are you crying? Are you alright?" Ferminity caught her breath and said, "I just saw," panting, "Christian and Suri kissing in the barn." The queen said, "Oh, I'm so sorry, sweetheart, it will be alright. Everything will be fine." "I'm sorry you made all these plans and spent all this money for nothing," said Ferminity. The queen said, "It's alright, darling, I will take care of everything, don't you worry one bit."

Ferminity went to find Suri to tell her she would not be marrying Christian, and he was all hers. She could have him for herself. She saw her walking up from the stable and said, "Christian is all yours. You can have him. The wedding is off". Suri said, "What are you talking about? I don't want Christian, I love Marcus." Ferminity said, "then why were you kissing Christian"? "I wasn't; I was kissing my boyfriend Marcus. He is Christian's twin brother there not identical but very close." "What Christian has a twin"? "Yes," said Suri, "and his name is Marcus, a lot different than Christian, I think." "Yes, I think you're right." "I am always right. I'm your best friend, and I could never do anything like that to you. I love you too much to do anything like that." "Yes I think you're right," "of course I'm right, I'm always right." They both started laughing. "Well, I better be going now that things are all cleared up. I'll see you later . Goodbye". Ferminity went back up to the castle and found her mother so she could explain everything. She told her what had happened. Her mother was relieved and continued working on the wedding.

The day had come, and everything was set. It looked beautiful. The flowers were exquisite. The cake had been made and was terrific. The decorations and most of all Ferminity she was in the most beautiful gown, her hair, her nails, her makeup every part of her looked incredible. She was gorgeous. Queen Azalia was wearing an elegant pink dress. She looked amazing when she came to the stairs. She met up with the King. He was wearing a tuxedo and looked very handsome. He kissed her cheek and asked, "are you ready"? She had a tear in her eye and said, "No, but I will have to be." Just then, Princess Ferminity came to the staircase looking beautiful. The King saw his little girl and began to cry at how she looked. She was no longer his little girl, she was a full-grown adult about to be married, and he had to say goodbye. How could he say goodbye to her? He knew he had to, so he took her hand and kissed her cheek, and said, "I love you, my beautiful little girl." Ferminity hugged her father and said, "I love you too, daddy."

They walked to the chapel, and the doors opened, and the guests rose to their feet. Queen Azailla walked in first, then Suri and Marcus, followed by Ferminity and King Leabou. Ferminity saw Christian standing at the end looking amazing with his brother standing next to him. They walked up the aisle, and Christian took Ferminitys hand, and the ceremony began. The Archbishop of Canterbury began to speak. The first thing he asked was, "Is there anyone here who thinks these two should not be married, speak now, or forever hold your peace?"

Everyone was silent, so he continued. He spoke about many things. He talked about the love between one another. He said many beautiful things that would come during their lives, the family they would create together, and their commitment to one another. Then they exchanged rings. The Archbishop asked, "Do you take this woman to be your lofty wedded wife?" Christian said, "I do with everything I am." And he asked Ferminity, "Do you take this man to be your lofty wedded husband?" "I do," she said, then he finished and said, "You may now kiss your bride."

Christian lifted her veil, and they began to kiss. This kiss was more passionate, more romantic, more in love than any other kiss they had ever given one another. They turned to face the crowd and began walking up the aisle. They reached the castle entrance, walked out, got into a beautifully decorated carriage, and rode down to a large building down the road where the reception would take place. Everything was magnificent: a large dance floor, a buffet with a ton of food, and a wonderful cake. Ferminity and Christian were in awe of what they saw. They began to dance, and the King came up behind Christian, tapped his shoulder, and said, "may I have this dance?" Christian said, "Of course," and he handed Ferminitys hand to the King. They danced their father-daughter dance, and he kissed her cheek and said, "I love you," she said, "I love you too, daddy." It began to get late Christian, and Ferminty went back to the carriage and left for their honeymoon.

They stayed in a beautiful hotel in Garlomania. The honeymoon suite. They had room service. They went outside and explored the village. When they finished, they went back to the hotel. The next day they put on their swimsuits and went to the pool. Christian went straight to the water. Ferminity laid on a towel to get a tan. But she forgot to put sunscreen on and fell asleep. She got burned. Luckily Christian noticed she was getting red and woke her up. They went back to the hotel room so Ferminity could put some aloe on it. "Christian," Ferminity said, "you go and look around. I'm not feeling very well right now. I just want to lay down and sleep. I won't be any fun for you". "Are you sure?" He said, "yes I'm sure." So he left to go exploring. Ferminity laid in the bed and went to sleep.

Christian went to a bunch of different shops. He was trying to find the perfect gift he could bring back to Ferminity. He was having a lot of trouble finding the ideal gift for her. There was one shop left. He went inside and started looking around. Then he saw it out of the corner of his eye. It was sparkling in the light from the window that was open in the back of the shop. He walked over to it. It was a beautiful diamond necklace on a golden chain. It was the most beautiful necklace he had ever seen. So he bought it for her.

He went back to the hotel and gave her the necklace. She loved it. She gave him a big hug and kiss and said thank you so much. He put it around her neck, and she got dressed, and they went to see a doctor that was in the village to see if he could give her something to help with the burn. He had a special burn ointment, especially for sunburns, and he gave it to her. She put it on and was immediately feeling better. So they went out for dinner. They had a wonderful meal. They finished their food, had some dessert, and went back to the hotel, and went to bed. The next day they went sightseeing together and saw many beautiful places. They spent the rest of their time together exploring everything. They went hiking and had a marvelous time. Three weeks had gone by, and their honeymoon was over, and they headed home.

When they got home, they had a surprise waiting for them. The King and Queen had built them a beautiful home they could live in and call their own. It was in the forest.

It was huge. It was like a mini castle. It had ten bedrooms, two kitchens, three living rooms, three family rooms, 12 bathrooms. They had thirty servants that took care of everything they would ever need. It was on ten thousand acres just for them.

There were three hot tubs in the backyard, five heated swimming pools, and a big horse track. There was a giant climbing wall. A vast stable where for Thunder and Midnight. Anything they could want, they had. They went back to the castle and thanked the King and Queen for their gifts. Then they came home and started playing with all their things. They played all day, and it began to get late, so they went inside and went to bed.

A year went by. Ferminity got pregnant. She told Christian he was so excited to be a father. He couldn't believe it was going to happen. Ferminity and Christian went up to the castle to tell her parents. The King had just gotten over the fact that his little girl was married to a stable boy now; that stable boy had gotten her pregnant and was making him a grandfather. He was not happy. Queen Azailla was so delighted and excited to be a grandmother.

Christian was so excited he was going to be a dad. He knew in his heart it would be a boy. Christian went and bought a pony. So he could teach his son to ride. He would have so much fun teaching him all the manly things he would need to know.

Queen Azailla decided to throw a baby shower for her daughter. Ferminity was able to invite all her friends from the Kingdom. They all came to her shower. She got lots of gifts for the baby. They played lots of games and had a wonderful time. While the ladies had the baby shower, King Leabou decided to get to know Christian. He took him on a hunting trip to a log cabin in the woods and began their adventure. They hunted for their food and sat around the campfire. They talked about what it would be with a little prince or princess running around the Kingdom. They had a wonderful time.

When King Leabou and Christian got back from their trip, Queen Azailla wanted to throw a grand ball. Because she was so excited to be a grandmother, and this time, it would be early enough, they wouldn't have to stop in the middle of the ball to have a baby in front of everyone. Queen Azailla started planning the ball; it would be bigger and better than any ball they had ever had.

Christian began making a nursery for the baby. He built a crib by hand and created a miniature play rocking horse to teach him to ride. He had everything a baby would ever need.

It was time for the ball to begin. Everyone was there, and everyone brought a small gift for the baby. But one man who no one knew had come to the ball. He walked up to the King and Queen and Ferminity and Christian and said, "Your Majestys, I am Lord Dulacne, Lord of Velangburg, the Kingdom that neighbors you. Unless you release the child to me now, when he reaches the age of sixteen, he will die, and there will be nothing you can do to stop it." "What do you want with my child?" Ferminity said, "You will soon find out; now release him to me." "But I'm still pregnant, and I won't allow you to take him from me even if I weren't." "Then you will both die." "Cease him," cried the King to the guards. As Ferminity fell to the ground, Christian ran to her side to try and help her. Then Lord Dulance Vanished, leaving a cloud of smoke behind. Ferminity began to sit up, and she was crying. "What are we going to do? We can't let him take away our baby". She said, "I don't know," said Christian, "I just don't know."

A few months went by, and it was getting close to Ferminity's due date. She was feeling fragile and tired from carrying all the baby's weight around for nine months. She was ready to pop. She and Sarah worked in the baby's room to add all the last-minute finishing touches that it would need. It began to get late, and Ferminity was getting very sleepy, so she said goodnight to Sarah. Sarah left, and Ferminity went to bed.

Princess Ferminity was having a tough time falling asleep; she could not get comfortable. She was having nightmares about Lord Dulance stealing her baby. Then all of a sudden, she felt something wet; her water had broken. She smacked Christian and said, "Wake up, we're having a baby" So Christian called for the doctor. He called for King Leabou and Queen Azailla to let them know it was time.

The doctor arrived just as ferminity was crowning. She was in labor for four hours. Finally, the moment came. The baby was here. They named him Prince Nicholi.

Christian was so excited. Finally, he had a son. Christian went and got a beautiful bouquet for Ferminity. He walked in, saw his wife, and said, "Well done, my love. How are you feeling? I am so proud of you. You did great." She said, "well, I'm still a little sore. Where is Nicholi?" Christian said, "they had to take him to run some tests and make sure he was alright and healthy." She asked, "when can I see him? Can you bring him to me Please?

Christian went to get the nurse. He asked, "when will you finished with all the tests." She told him, "in half an hour, I will bring him to you." So Christian went back to

Ferminity and told her to get some rest. It would be a little bit before he was ready. So ferminity decided to take a little nap. Just as she closed her eyes, Queen Azailla walked in. Ferminity opened her eyes and said, "Hello, when did you get here"? The queen said, "Hello, my darling. I am so proud of you. You did a fantastic job. Where is my grandson? I'm sure he is as gorgeous as me and handsome as your father." She giggled. "I'm sure he is," said Ferminity. As she reached for her mother, she asked, "Where is father"? "He is coming. I wanted to come in first and see how you were". She motioned the King to come in. He said, "Hello baby, how are you?" She said, "I'm ok. I just wish they would let me see Nicholi. Where's Christian?" "He's coming. He just had to pick something up real; quick."

When Christian got back, he had a handful of balloons in one hand and Nicholi in the other hand. "Hello there, I think someone here wants to meet his mommy." Ferminity sat up and reached for Nicholi. She held him tight and kissed his cheek. Then she whispered in his ear, "Here's my little boy. I love you so much." He's so beautiful. I don't know how I lived so long without him. When can we go home?" She asked the nurse. "Today, as soon as you speak with the doctor. He will be with you in a little bit." "Thank you," said Ferminity as she sat up and began nursing Nicholi. An hour passed, and Christian fell asleep in a chair. Ferminity laid Nicholi down next to her and fell asleep.

The next day Ferminity was able to go home. When they got there, they took Nicholi up to the nursery and laid him in his crib. Then came downstairs, went outside to see Thunder and Shera. She hadn't been able to ride while pregnant. She was excited to get back on again. Christian got on Shera, and Ferminty got on Thunder, and they began to ride. They rode for about an hour, then came back and went to check on Nicholi. When they walked into the nursery, Nicholi was beginning to wake up. Ferminity picked him up and went downstairs. She took Nicholi outside and introduced him to Thunder and Sherra. After all, he was a prince, and he would need to be able to ride. When Nicholi saw the horses, his eyes lit up with excitement. She got on Thunder and held the rein with one hand and Nicholi with the other hand. She let Nicholi hold the reins with his tiny little hands. He was so cute he had a big smile on his face. They rode all around the forest.

Femininity took Nicholi into the house. Christian and dinner were ready and waiting for them. They ate their meal, and Ferminity and Christian took Nicholi up for his bath. He loved playing in the water with all his little boats and ships. They took him out, and got him all dry, and put his pajamas on. And put him to bed. They laid him in his crib, held each other, and watched as he slowly drifted off to sleep. As he slept, they slowly crept out of his room, closing the door behind them.

They went to the living room, and Ferminity sat on the couch. Christian got a book from the shelf sat next to Ferminity. As she leaned against him, he began to read to her. As Christian was reading, they heard a noise coming from Nicholi's room. They got up and went upstairs to check on him, and he was there, Lord Dulance standing over Nicholi's crib. Ferminity screamed and passed out with shock. Then Christian said, "what are you doing here"? Lord Dulance said, "I've come for the baby, he is mine now, and I will take him with me." Christian yelled for the guards and ran to get his son. As he ran toward the crib, Lord Dulance raised his hand shouted a curse. Christian froze in his step. Lord Dulance picked up Nicholi and vanished in a cloud of smoke. As he disappeared, Christian was released from the spell. He went to the crib he saw his son was gone.

He bent down to help Ferminity wake up, and she said, "Where is Nicholi?" Christian said, "he is gone, but I will get him back. I promise you I will not stop until we have our son in our arms again. And Christian left to go to the castle to let King Leabou and Queen Azailla know what had happened and see if they could help.

He went to the throne room of King Leabou and said, "Your majesty, Lord Dulance, has kidnapped Prince Nicholi. I need your help to find him." King Leabou rose to his feet and said, "Call all the knights and guards and raise an army. We will attack the Kingdom of Velanburg now to get my grandson back. Call all the weapon makers we attack at first light". They began to get ready. Christian could not wait for them. He went to the armory, put on some armor, grabbed a sword and shield, then went to the stable to get Midnight. As he got Midnight saddled up. Ferminity walked into the stable. She gave him a good luck kiss and said, "bring home our baby." Then Christian said, "I will," and he rode off into the night.

By 4:00 am the following day, King Leabou's army was ready to attack; they got on their horses and rode off to the Kingdom of Valangburg, with King Leabou leading the charge. When they caught up with Christian, he had been planning a way into the castle. When the army was outside Valangburgs walls there, guards were alerted. And they began to attack. While the army was fighting in front of the castle. Christian showed King Leabou a secret entrance he had found in the back of the castle. King Leabou and a few of the King's guards went to the private door while the army fought in the front. They snuck into the castle and tried to find Prince Nicholi. They went to the tallest tower in the Kingdom and heard a faint crying sound. Christian slashed the door with his sword, and it fell open. He went in, and Nicholi was lying on an altar in the center of the room. Lord Dulance was standing over a cauldron, adding ingredients and saying a spell in a different language.

Christian charged in and headed straight for Lord Dulance. As Christian charged him, Lord Dulance raised his hand and cast a spell. Christian was thrown against the wall and knocked unconscious. King Leabou was behind Christian, and Lord Dulance had not seen him yet as Lord Dulance went to Christian to finish him off. King Leabou charged Lord Dulance and stabbed him in the chest. Lord Dulance fell to the ground and died in an instant. King Leabou went to Christian and helped him up, and Christian said, "thank you, your highness." King Leabou said with a smile, "you can call me father or dad whatever you want. You are my son". He said, "thank you, father," and they went to the altar to get Prince Nicholi.

As Christian picked up little Nicholi, he had a big smile on his face. Christian hugged his son and said, "I love you so much, Nicholi." Then they began walking out of the room.

As they were walking down the stairs, Lord Dulances guards were racing up the stairs. King Leabou pulled out his sword and began fighting them off to protect his grandson. They made it halfway down, and king Leabou was stabbed in the side as the final guard was dropping. As he began to fall, Christian went to him, grabbed his arm, and put it over his left shoulder while carrying Nicholi in his right arm. They made it out of the secret entrance and to their horses.

Christian got King Leabou onto his horse, then Christian got on his horse with Nicholi. Then they rode back to the Kingdom of Morane. When they got there, the King was unconscious due to blood loss. Christian took Thunder to the stable and walked the King on his horse and Nicholi up to the castle door. When they got there, Queen Azailla and Princess Ferminity were in the lobby passing. Ferminity saw Christian holding Nicholi and holding onto her father's reins. She ran to Nicholi, grabbed him, and hugged him. Then kissed his little cheek and asked if he was alright. Then she saw her father bent over and bleeding. Queen Azailla ran to King Leabou, Christian helped him from the horse, and walked him to the couch. Queen Azailla got some cloth to stop the bleeding and called for the doctor at once. When the doctor arrived, he stitched up King Leabou and recommend staying in bed for a week to recover.

Ferminity went to her father's bed with Nicholi in her arms. She said, "thank you so much for bringing Nicholi back to me father. I don't know what I would have done without him." "You are welcome, my darling. I love you so much, and I love that little boy." Ferminity smiled and handed Nicholi to his grandfather. He smiled and cooed the cutest little coo. King Leabou kissed his little cheek then Ferminity left her father's room so he could get some rest.

Ferminity took Nicholi back home. When she got there, Christian was getting out of the shower. He got dressed and came downstairs. He picked up his little boy from Ferminity's arms, kissed his cheek, and said, "no one will ever harm you again as long as I live."

The following day Ferminity, Christian, and Nicholi went up to the castle to check on the King. When they got to his room, many nurses and doctors were working on the King. They were not allowed to go in, and Queen Azailla was outside the room crying. "What happened" Cried Ferminity? "He had a stroke. They don't know if he will be alright." "Oh no," cried Ferminity. She was so upset. Christian took her in his arms and said, "it will be alright. He will be fine." Ferminity handed Nicholi to Christian and went and hugged her mother.

A few hours had passed. Queen Azailla and Ferminity, and Christian were in the dining room having some lunch. The doctor came in and said, "I am sorry it does not look good. I don't think he will make it through the night." They went to his room. The King was sleeping; they all stood around his bed and said their goodbyes. Ferminity kissed her father on the cheek and said, "I love you so much. I will miss you always and forever." The queen walked up to him, kissed him, and said, You are my forever love, and I will love you forever and always. Goodbye, my love." Then Christian said, "thank you, Father, for giving me a family. Goodbye".

As Christian said goodbye, King Leabou's heart stopped, and he stopped breathing. The queen was so upset. She held his hand and laid on his stomach, crying until the doctors said it was time to leave. As they all walked out of the room, they turned back and said one last goodbye. And the King was gone. As ferminity and her mother walked through the halls of the castle, they began to cry as they thought of all the memories they had with King Leabou.

King Leabou was a great man. And the queen wanted him to have a wonderful funeral. She had a magnificent coffin made. The casket was put on a carriage full of flowers. All the King's horses pulled it through the Kingdom. All the King's guards rode behind in their armor, all polished. They were on horses in rows of six. Queen Azailla and Princess Ferminity, Christian and Prince Nicholi rode together in an open carriage. They rode through the whole Kingdom until they reached the cemetery. When they arrived, they exited the carriage and proceeded to the burial site. They had a beautiful ceremony for the King. The whole Kingdom had come to pay their respects to the great King who was loved by all. They all had flowers to lay at the site. As King Leabou was laid to rest, the guards pulled their swords out, forming a canopy for Queen Azailla And Ferminity and Christian and Nicholi to proceed back to the carriage. As they turned to walk back, they saw the whole Kingdom coming together, and they smiled and waved to them all. As they entered the carriage and began to head back to the castle, a little girl ran up to the carriage. She handed the queen arose and said," May God bless you." The queen took the flower, smiled, and said, "thank you, my dear."

They proceeded back to the palace. The queen walked up the giant staircase to the main door and entered the castle alone. Ferminity, Christian, and Nicholi arrived at their home. They went in, and Ferminity looked at Christian and said, "I don't think she should be left alone in that big castle." Christian said, "you're right; she shouldn't be alone at a time like this." "Maybe we should move into the castle with her." "That's a good idea, so they packed their bags, loaded them in the carriage, and rode up to the castle. As they entered the castle, they began looking for the queen. When they found her, she was sitting in the throne room alone, hunched over with her head in her hands, crying and holding on to the rose the child from the village had given her. Ferminity ran to her, hugged her, and said, "It's alright, mother. I'm here for you, so you won't have to be alone. We are going to move in with you and take care of you."

The queen looked up and said, "It's alright, dear, that is not what is going to happen. Next week we will have a coronation ceremony, and Christian will be crowned King of Morane, and you will be crowned Queen of Morane. You too will be taking over the Kingdom." "What"? "That is what happens when a king dies. The next of kin take over the throne. And you are the Princess, so you are next in line to be queen." "Oh my," said Ferminity, "I can't be queen, I am not ready, and you are queen." "I will always be queen, but my time is up now that your father is gone. The Kingdom needs two rulers: a king and a queen." "But what will happen to you?" "I will be one of your many subjects. I will move out of the palace and find a quiet place of my own where my grandchildren can visit me." "Oh, mother, I don't think I can be queen." You have no choice, darling. It is your birthright." "Oh, mother, I guess I should go let

Christian know what is going on and know he is going to be king."

Ferminity left the throne room and went to find Christian and Nicholi. Christian and Nicholi were in the lobby waiting for Ferminity. Ferminity said, "Christian, I need to speak with you about something significant." Christian looked concerned and said, "what is it? Is your mother alright?" "Yes, she is just despondent about losing father, and next week she won't be Queen any longer." "Why won't she be Queen?" Asked Christian. "Because I will be Queen, and you will be King." "What"? Asked Christian, "Yes, now that father is gone, the kingdom needs to have a king and a queen." "Oh my." Said Christian, "and since you're a princess, that means you're next in line to be queen." "That's right, and we will be the King and Queen of Morane." "Oh my," said Christian.

The following week arrived very quickly. It was time for the coronation ceremony. The queen was in the throne room alone, ready to give up her crown. The crowd came in and sat down for the ceremony. Ferminity and Christian were getting their best outfits on that a new king and queen should wear. It was time for the ceremony. The queen was sitting on her throne for the last time. She stood as the door opened. Princess Ferminity took Christian's hand, and they began walking down the aisle.

As Queen Azailla watched her only daughter walk down the aisle to take her place as queen, she smiled and whispered in Ferminity's ear, "I wish your father were here to see this." As she took the crown from her head and handed it to the Archbishop of Canterbury, she bowed her title away. The Archbishop Of Canterbury placed the crown on Princess Ferminitys head and said, "I dub thee Queen Ferminity Queen of Morane." Then he took the Kings Crown from the throne, and Christian knelt in front of him. And he said, "I dub thee King Christian of Morane" He placed the crown on his head. Then Queen Ferminity and King Christian turned to face the audience, and everyone cheered for them. They sat on their thrones as the new King and Queen.

Queen Azailla was so proud of her daughter, the new Queen of Morane. After the ceremony finished, they went into a giant ballroom where the whole Kingdom had been invited to dinner to celebrate the coronation. King Christian and Queen Ferminity sat at the head of the room where her mother and father would sit during events. They enjoyed an excellent meal. Then it was over. They said their goodbyes to all the guests as they left. Then the castle was quiet again except for the sounds of everything being cleaned up and Nicholi making noise. Queen Azailla left the castle for the last time. She was no longer queen, so she went to a little cottage in the village close enough to visit her daughter, the new queen, and her grandson. Ferminity and Christian went up the stairs and put Nicholi to bed, and then they went to bed as the new King and Queen of Morane.